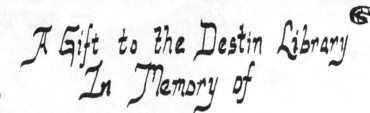

A Gift to the Destin Library
In Memory of

CAPT. BUD PERRY

from

The Sound Restaurant Friends

4/95

For Tom, Abigail, and Imogen   G. A.

For Mark, Elise, Bernard, and Marc   B. W.

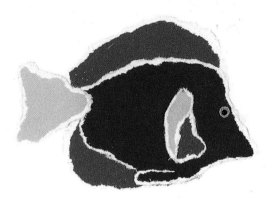

First published in the United States 1993
by Dial Books for Young Readers
A Division of Penguin Books USA Inc.
375 Hudson Street | New York, New York 10014
Published in Great Britain 1992
by Simon & Schuster Young Books
Text copyright © 1992 by Georgie Adams
Pictures copyright © 1992 by Brigitte Willgoss
All rights reserved | Printed in Belgium
First Edition
10 9 8 7 6 5 4 3 2 1

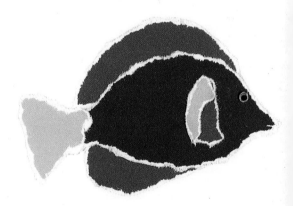

Library of Congress Cataloging in Publication Data
Adams, Georgie. Fish fish fish | by Georgie Adams ;
pictures by Brigitte Willgoss.
p. cm.
Summary: Colorful collage illustrations introduce
various sizes and shapes of fish.
ISBN 0-8037-1208-1 (tr)
1. Fishes—Juvenile literature.   [1. Fishes.]
I. Willgoss, Brigitte, ill.   II. Title.
QL617.2.A33 1993 597—dc20 91-43748 CIP AC

Fish Fish Fish

picture... ...s ...s

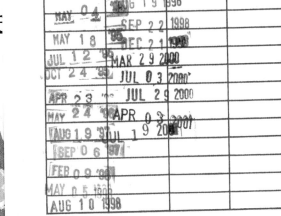

Dial Books for Young Readers New York

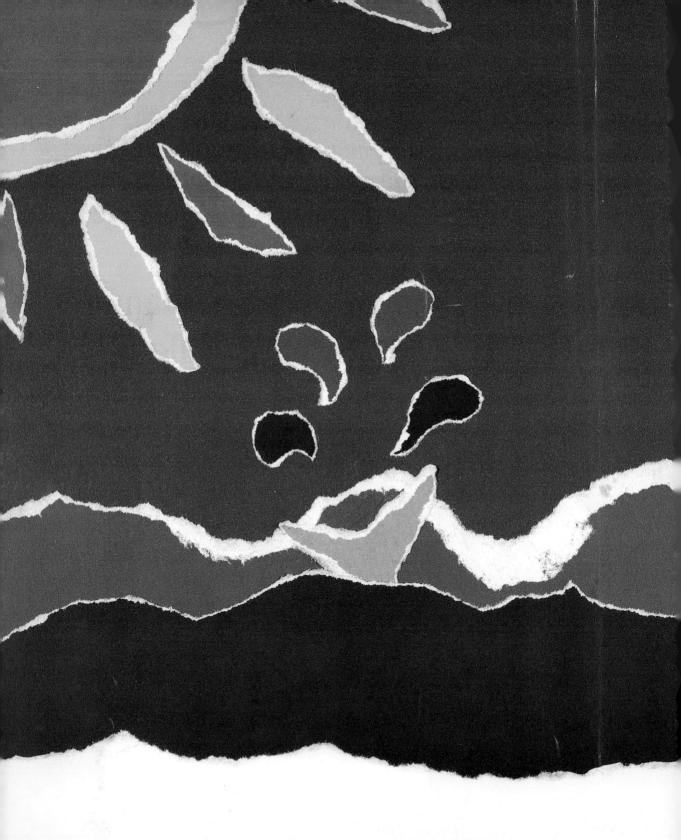

Look in the oceans, look in the seas.

What will you find? Fish, fish, fish!

Look in rivers and lakes and streams.

What will you find? Fish, fish, fish!

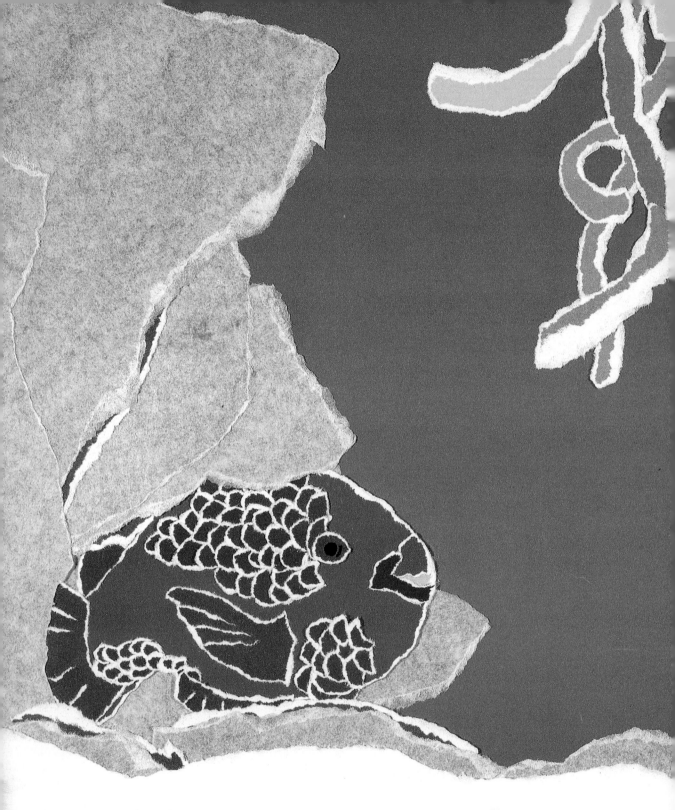

All fish have gills for breathing
and fins and tails for swimming.

And most fish have scales
that make them waterproof.

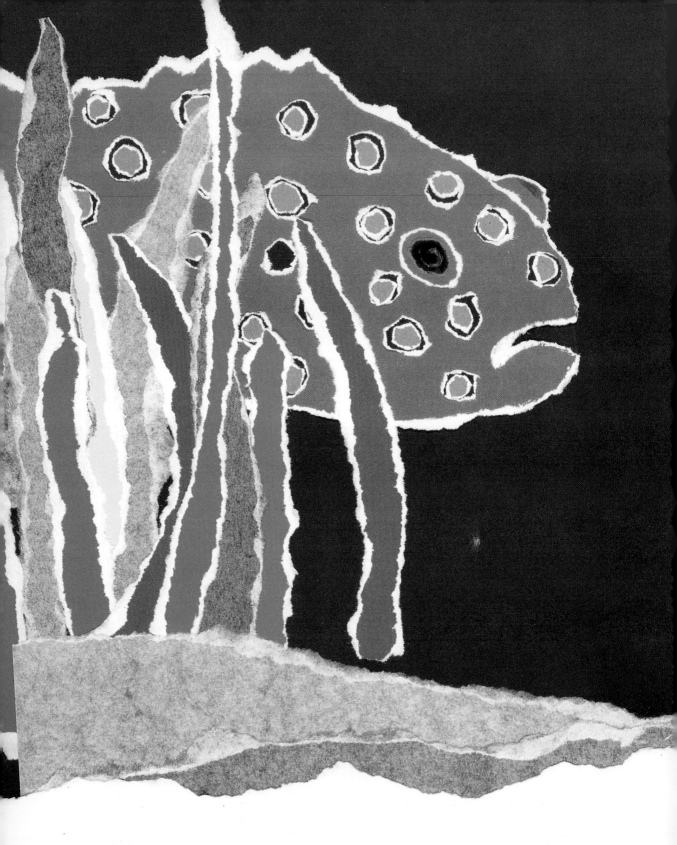

Fish come in all colors.

Some have spots of black or blue.

Some have stripes of black and white,

or yellow, orange, and gray.

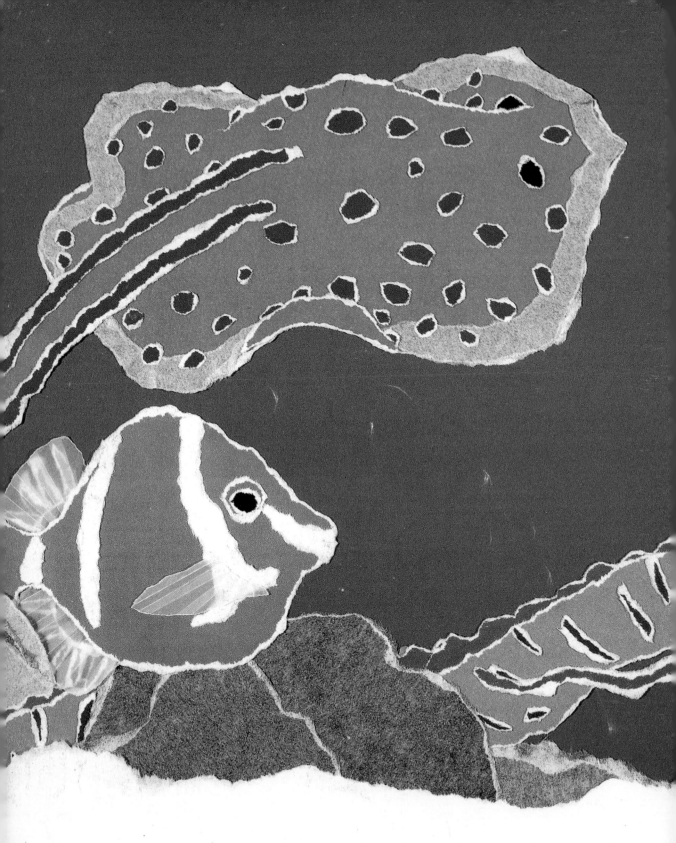

Fish come in all shapes too. . . .

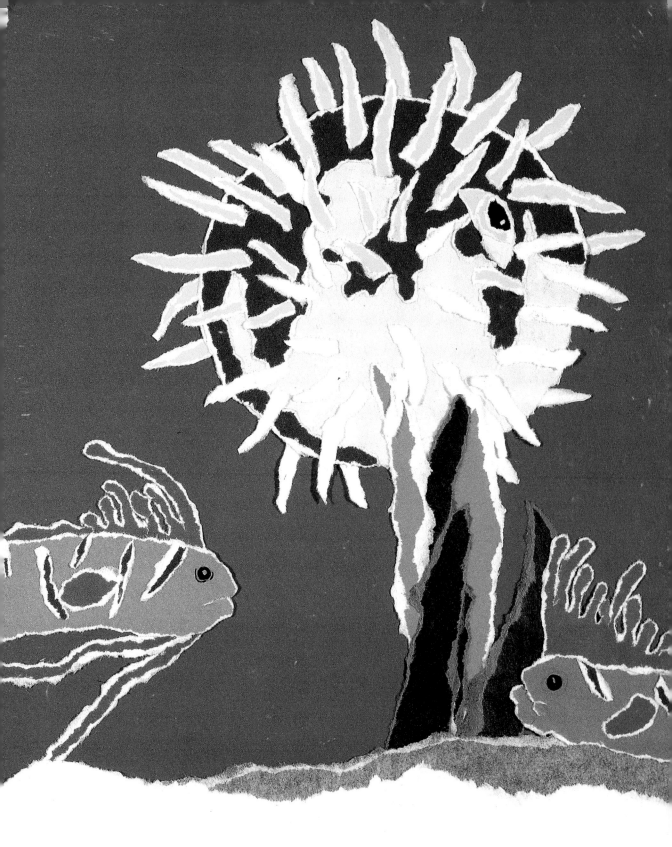

Flat, round, skinny, and fat.

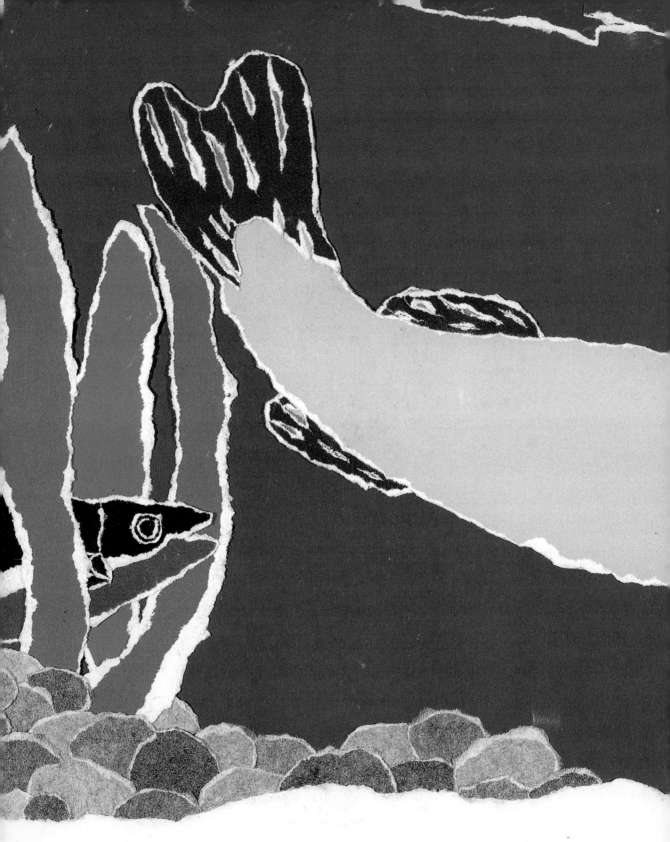

There are fish that are fierce

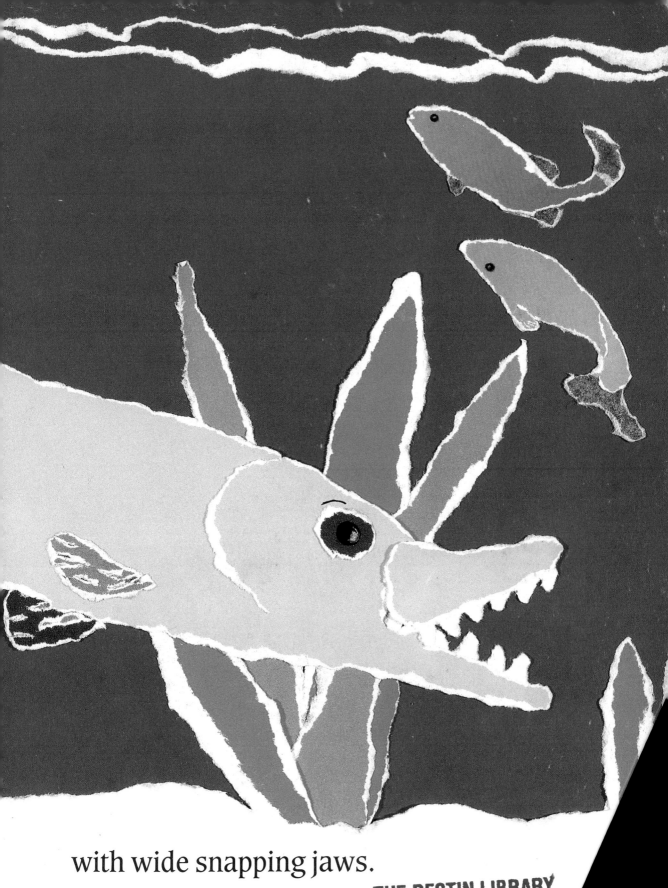

with wide snapping jaws.

...s are gentle

with mouths that look ready for kisses.

fish are big and bold

and are better left alone.

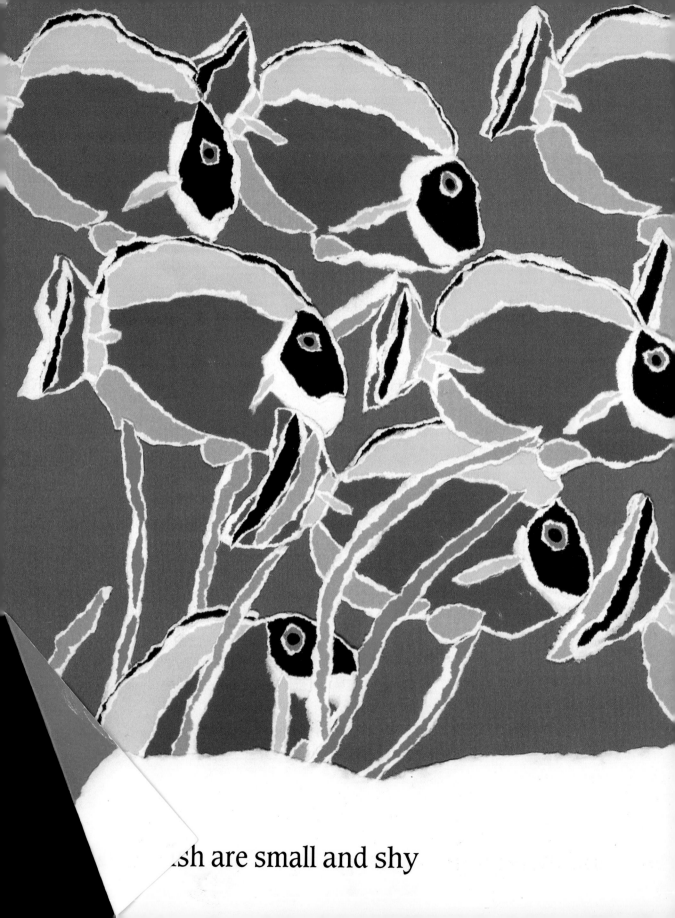

...sh are small and shy

and swim together in groups called schools.

There are fish that always stay
at the bottom of the sea,

and fish that take leaps and fly
over the waves.

Swimming, feeding, hiding, sleeping in streams, rivers, lakes, oceans, seas. . . .

If the waters stay pure and clean,
there will always be fish, fish, fish!

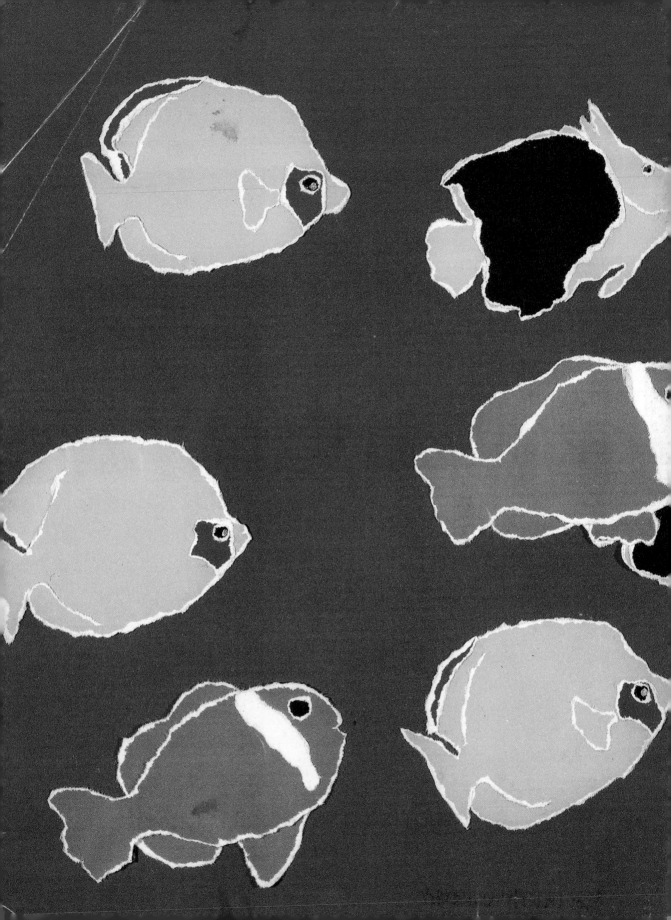